the mine

THE TRAPPS FAMILY ADVENTURES

THE MINE

By LAWRENCE E. R. ADAMS

Illustrations by ROBERT G. ADAMS

TRAPPS PUBLISHING

THE PUBLISHER:
Trapps Publishing
P.O. Box 212
Irricana, Alberta, Canada T0M 1B0

Library and Archives Canada Cataloguing in Publication

Adams, Lawrence E. R. (Lawrence Edward Roy), 1941-
    The mine / by Lawrence E.R. Adams ; illustrations by Robert G. Adams.

(The Trapps family adventures)
Includes some text in Inuktitut..
ISBN 978-0-9781532-9-8

    I. Adams, Robert G. (Robert Godon), 1968-
II. Title. III. Series: Adams, Lawrence E. R. (Lawrence Edward Roy), 1941- . Trapps family adventures.

PS8601.D454M56 2011   jC813'.6   C2011-903264-3

Cover: Robert G. Adams
Printing: Houghton Boston

DISCLAIMER

All the characters in this book are fictitious; any similarity between any persons living or deceased is merely a coincidence.

AWARDS

"THE OLD ONE," the first book in, **"THE TRAPPS FAMILY ADVENTURES,"** series, was awarded the silver medal for Canada-West-Best Regional Fiction at the 12th Annual Independent Publisher Book Awards in Los Angeles on 30th May 2008.

For the "Gang"

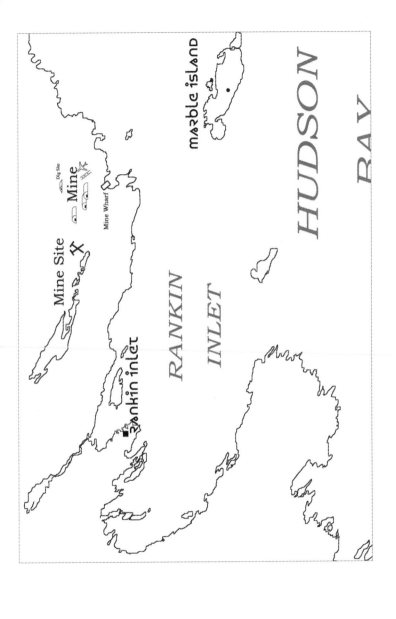

CONTENTS

PROLOGUE 9

THE TERRAIN HAS CHANGED 13

THERE'S NO PLACE LIKE HOME 21

WE'RE READY; LET'S GO 29

ARE WE THERE YET? 33

SAFETY FIRST 36

WE'RE READY; LET'S RIDE 45

THE MINE 52

THE PIT 57

MY HEAD HURTS 63

A RACE AGAINST TIME 75

THE MILL 79

YOU FOUND US 89

GLOSSARY 92

ACKNOWLEDGMENTS 93

PROLOGUE

It wasn't the call of the North that brought the Trapps family to the vast treeless region of Canada's North, known as the Tundra. This trip was not going to be anything as romantic as the, "call of the north" evoked; this wasn't even going to be a holiday. Numerous hours of backbreaking work would dominate the expedition, or so they thought.

Max Trapps, a world-class archaeologist, had led expeditions to numerous places in the world conducting excavations to uncover the secrets of the past. Now he had been chosen to conduct an archaeological dig at an ancient Inuit settlement. Workers at the Blue Diamond Mine, approximately thirty kilometres northeast of Rankin Inlet on the west shore of Hudson Bay in the Northwest Territories, made the discovery while working near their airstrip. Throughout the dig, the mining company generously agreed to supply the food and lodgings for the entire Trapps family.

When Amy Trapps and her brothers Ty and Parker meet "THE OLD ONE," secrets and mysteries of the north and the Inuit way of life will be laid bare before them. Nothing they could have done before leaving their home in Calgary could have prepared them for the adventures they are about to experience. They will enter an environment that few people have ever seen and even fewer will ever live in. It is a harsh and unforgiving land that holds untold beauty and adventure for those who dare to accept its challenges.

The north is home for the Inuit, the only race of humans who are able to live under its conditions without assistance from the outside world. Their ability to adapt to their environment allows them to reap the bounty of the north. Only the most adventurous and well-equipped explorer has been able to penetrate the Inuit's habitat and lived to tell about it.

Amy's curiosity and thirst for knowledge sometimes get her into jams that only her brothers can help resolve. She enjoys assisting her father during an excavation and likes nothing better than to uncover a relic from the past and unlock its secrets.

Ty is twelve, one year younger than Amy, and a gifted athlete. His favourite sport is hockey, and if allowed to he would play it twenty-four hours a day.

Parker, one year younger than Ty, doesn't possess his brother's athletic abilities, but his determination to succeed and not be outdone by anyone makes him a worthy opponent. He possesses a photographic memory, which has proven to be an asset when his sister gets them involved in one of her many schemes.

After meeting the shaman Kadluk (the adults know him as THE OLD ONE), the kids now have the ability to communicate through their Inuas, a gift that is only bestowed upon a shaman. An Inua is the spiritual occupant, or spirit helper, who resides in all living and inanimate things.

The amulet the kids found at the dig is the amulet that was made by the first shaman. When they wear it, it provides them protection from anything that might otherwise harm them, and since it has the ability to replicate itself, each one of the kids has their own amulet and receives its protection.

Chapter 1

The Terrain Has Changed

Kadluk had returned home the night before from his trapline. Upon rising from his bed, as was his custom, he walked outside to check the weather. How it felt would have a profound effect on what he would do that day.

It was early morning and still dark, as it always was this time of year. He felt the wind gently touch his face and faintly heard Sila, the wind deity, telling someone about a coming storm. She was saying she would be busy ensuring the wind was kept to sufficient force to allow a full-blown blizzard to build. It would be coming from the north, but when it would strike or where, she didn't say.

"Sila, where and when is the storm going to strike?" Kadluk asked through his Inua.

There was no reply; only the gentle caress of the wind was present.

Again Kadluk called, *"Sila, where and when is the storm going to strike?"*

He stood alone in the silence that surrounded him. Not a noise could be heard. Kadluk knew it was futile to keep calling Sila, as sometimes she would answer and sometimes she wouldn't. He made a mental note to listen for any further information about the storm. A blizzard was not something to trifle with. Although it was a mere inconvenience to Kadluk, to others it was a disaster with dire consequences for the ill prepared.

His mind wandered to his young Kabloona friends. They, of course, would still be sleeping. They never rose as early as he did. He would look in on them later when he again checked on the storm Sila had talked about.

He entered his house to make the piping hot tea with liberal spoonfuls of sugar that he so relished. So far the day held promise, and if the weather held, it would be very enjoyable to skin and stretch the hides of the animals he had harvested from his trapline.

*   *   *

When the opportunity presented itself, the kids were quick to take advantage. After all, it wasn't often they took a day off from home schooling or helping at the dig their father Max was conducting.

Before dawn in the half light, the kids were riding their skidoos westward towards the small lake where the miners liked to fish during their time off. During November, daylight is at a premium. Less than four hours of sunlight a day are observed. The sun rises after 10:00 a.m. and sets before 2:00 p.m. It is therefore imperative to make the most of the daylight hours.

The sun was up when they arrived at the lake. Ty was riding the lead skidoo, followed closely by Amy and Parker on the second skidoo. With the lake frozen over and very little snow covering it, the ice made a fun surface to race on. It was easy to lose traction and hard to get up any speed unless you started slowly, allowing the track to bite into the ice and slowly gain speed. Once speed was gained, it was fun to get the skidoos spinning out of control. It reminded the kids of the rides they had enjoyed at the carnival in the past.

Ty's skidoo appeared to have better traction than Amy's and Parker's. He came out of the skids quicker and seemed to have better traction while accelerating.

"Race you to the other shore!" Ty yelled as he gunned his skidoo and took off.

"Go faster, Amy! Give it more gas!" Parker yelled as Ty sped away.

"I'm going as fast as I can. Can't you feel the track slipping on the ice?" Amy replied.

"Well, go faster anyway; he's getting away from us!" Parker howled as Ty raced across the lake.

When Ty reached the far shore, he stopped and waited for them to catch up.

"What took you so long?" he asked with a big grin on his face.

"Your track is probably newer. You have better traction than us," Amy stated.

"No excuses," Ty said. "I beat you fair and square."

"Trade us machines and we'll race you back across the lake and then we'll see who's the fastest," Parker challenged.

"Now, now, don't be a spoiled sport. It was a fair race and I won." Ty chided his little brother while basking in the glory of a win.

"Ty's right. He won fair and square. Let's go back to the other side and eat lunch. We're fast running out of daylight, and then we'll head for home," Amy informed her brothers.

"Sounds good to me," Ty yelled as he gunned his engine and his skidoo shot forward.

"Hurry, Amy," Parker howled. "He's getting away!"

Ty's action had caught them off guard and he had a considerable lead before they got underway.

"I should have known he'd do something like that," Amy shouted to Parker.

"Yeah, now we'll never catch him. Look at the lead he's got already," Parker remarked in disgust.

When Amy and Parker neared the shore, there was Ty with a big grin on his face.

"Get the grub out; I'm starved. Winning all these races makes a man hungry," he advised his siblings.

"Jiminy-Willie-Peppers. Maybe if it had been a fair race you wouldn't have won," Parker whined. He was getting excited; he didn't like to lose anymore than Ty did.

"Now, now little brother, don't be a sore loser," Ty chided Parker again.

17

Amy quickly unpacked the sandwiches and they were soon eating and enjoying the hot cocoa from the thermos. The temperature was -23C, but the kids were used to this temperature and didn't really feel the cold anymore unless it was below -35C. They ate their lunch in silence, enjoying the beautiful panorama that lay before them, careful to keep their skin from being exposed to the cold air.

"Amy, where's the amulet? I don't see it," Ty suddenly asked as he looked at Amy. "You didn't forget it, did you?"

"Yes. It was on the dresser, but in our rush to leave, I forgot to pick it up," Amy replied.

"It's okay, Amy. We don't need it. We're just going for a skidoo ride. What could possibly happen?" Parker piped in.

"Yeah, you're probably right. What could happen?" Ty remarked to no one in particular, as if he were talking to himself. Then he added, "But you know, since we found it at the dig, it has saved us from so many dangers. It really is our good luck charm, and it's comforting to have it with us."

*   *   *

"Remember the first day we arrived? Remember how we felt when we first saw the tundra?" Amy asked through her Inua, not wanting to break the silence she was enjoying, but wanting to get the conversation away from the amulet. She was embarrassed about forgetting it and didn't want to be reminded about it again.

Since Kadluk had shown them how to communicate through their Inuas, the kids had often used this course of communication to converse with each other while still enjoying the tranquillity of the environment. No one except a shaman would know they were communicating.

"Well, I for one can't believe what has happened since we arrived," Ty blurted out. *"When I first saw the tundra through the windows of the plane, I thought, 'Lord help us; we've come to the most desolate and boring place on earth.' When I think of how flat and treeless the terrain looked, only broken by patches of lakes and rivers, I can't even begin to express how I felt. Amy, when you were so excited about new adventures that lay ahead, I thought you had gone bonkers. I couldn't see anything to get excited about, and when we circled the mine and our airstrip, I thought we had come to the end of the earth."*

"I always try to remember what Dad said - 'Very few things are as they at first seem to be,'" Amy reminded her brothers.

"I remember that." Parker, not wanting to be left out of the conversation, piped in with his two cents' worth. *"I remember you two arguing about the terrain on the plane. Mom and Dad were quite amused by your antics. I made up my mind right then and there to wait and see what would happen. I thought, 'Time will tell what lies ahead, and then we'll see who's right.'"*

"Well, I'm glad it was Amy who was right. This trip has been one adventure after the other. What was it Mr. Munro said when he opened the aircraft door?" Ty asked no one in particular.

"He said, 'Welcome to the mine. I'm Bob Munro, the mine superintendent, and your host for the duration of your stay,'" Parker replied.

"Yeah, that's it, that's exactly what he said. He made me feel at home as soon as he said it. Although at the time, I still felt we had landed at the most boring place on earth. We're sure lucky he's in charge of the mine," Ty advised his siblings.

chapter ii

there's no place like home

Amy said to no one in particular, *"Remember how naive we were when we arrived? When I look back now, we must have sounded really inexperienced to Mr. Munro. Like when I asked why those oil barrels were beside the road with rods sticking out of them."*

"Yeah, and before he could answer, I shouted out that the rods were connected by ropes," Ty recalled.

"Well, he did say it was a good question, and then he explained that they were there in case of a blizzard or whiteout and the ropes ended at a building. In an emergency, a person could follow along the ropes to the safety of a building," Parker offered in explanation.

"I realize that now, Parker," Amy remarked.

"*That wasn't the best part, Amy. The best part was when you said, 'Aren't a blizzard and a whiteout the same thing, Mr. Munro?' And then he said, 'No, dear, a blizzard is a snowstorm with winds blowing over fifty-six kilometres an hour with visibility less than four hundred metres for three hours or more. Sometimes a blizzard is described as a heavy snowstorm with high winds. A whiteout is a polar weather condition that occurs when the amount of light coming through a cloud equals the amount of light that is being reflected off the snow on the ground. When this happens, it is impossible to distinguish features on the ground because everything appears to be white with no depth,'*" Parker shouted.

"Go ahead and laugh, Mr. Smarty-pants. Not everyone has a photographic memory like you do," Amy playfully shot back at her younger brother.

Parker was having great fun at Amy's expense and was really enjoying the friendly banter with his siblings.

Ty and Parker continued the friendly chitchat back and forth, recalling the events as they happened. Amy was experiencing something different as she listened to her brothers. Her mind began to wander, and in her mind's eye she could recall that day's events as they had unfolded.

*   *   *

After Mr. Munro explained the difference between a blizzard and a whiteout, she recalled the following events:

"Jiminy-Willie-Peppers, I wouldn't want to be caught in one of those!" exclaimed Parker.

"They're not very pleasant to be in. I've been in a few of them, and it's very nerve-wracking. Believe me. The snow feels like a million needles hitting your exposed flesh. I don't know anyone who enjoys the mind-numbing wind-chill or the afterglow of frostbite," Mr. Munro informed the group.

"I've never before heard it put quite like that, but I'll take your word for it, Bob," their father, Max, said to their host.

The mine buildings seemed to grow out of the ground as the vehicle carrying the group drew nearer.

"What's that big building, Mr. Munro?" Amy wanted to know, pointing at the long low building that was expanding in size as they approached.

"That's the kitchen; that's where we eat all our meals. That small building behind it is the storage shed for the kitchen. The next three smaller buildings are residences, and the larger one at the end is the bunkhouse for the staff. The first residence is mine, and the second one will be the one you'll be staying in," Mr. Munro informed the group.

"Ah, home sweet home!" Ty muttered to himself.

The group rode in silence, staring at the buildings that appeared to be sitting in the middle of a rock pile with scant vegetation.

Ty was the first to speak. "Is this it? Is this all there is to this place?" he asked, looking from left to right.

"Ty don't be rude!" Amy snapped.

"I'm not being rude, but there's nothing here. We're going to spend the next six months in the middle of nowhere!" Ty wailed.

"There's more to the mine than just these buildings, isn't there, Mr. Munro?" Parker inquired.

"There sure is, young fellow; these are just the kitchen and the living quarters. The mine itself is about a kilometre west of here over that ridge," Mr. Munro said, pointing in the direction of the road that led to the west.

"See Ty; there's lots more to the mine. We'll have lots to do," Amy happily exclaimed.

"Yeah, right!" Ty mumbled.

*   *   *

Amy was again aware of her brothers talking and thought to herself, 'Why did I recall what happened when we first arrived?' She dismissed it, although it had been a pleasant flashback, as she listened to Parker say to Ty, "Remember you asked Mr. Munro when we could ride the quads and skidoos. He said, 'Once you pass the required safety course you can ride them and not before.' I remember the disappointed look on your face; you just sat back and didn't say anything else. Remember?" Parker chuckled as he recalled the event.

"Come on, you two; finish up and let's get going. It'll be dark before we get home," Amy advised her brothers.

The boys were packed up and ready to go in jig time. Ty had already started his skidoo when Parker, upon casting a longing look at the faraway hill on the other side of the lake, shouted, "What's that?"

"What's what?" queried Ty, turning in the direction Parker was looking.

"I don't see anything," remarked Amy as she looked towards the hill.

"I seen an animal on that hill," shouted Parker.

"Yeah, right. I don't see anything. I think you're seeing things," Ty snapped.

"Come on, you two; we've got to go," Amy remarked as she started her skidoo.

"No, really. I did see an animal. It just walked around the hill." Parker pleaded to be believed.

"Well, it's probably just a caribou and we've seen lots of them," Amy sternly remarked.

"You're probably right; let's go," Ty replied.

"It might have been a caribou, but I think it was a musk ox," Parker retorted indignantly.

That got Ty's attention. A caribou was one thing, but a musk ox was something else. The kids hadn't seen a real muskox in the wild, and he wasn't going to pass up the chance of seeing one.

"We'd better check this out. It won't take long!" he shouted as he gunned his engine. The skidoo sprang to life and he tore across the lake.

"Quick, Amy! Catch Ty; he's getting away!" Parker howled.

"You two; I don't know why I listen to you; you never listen to me," Amy scolded her brother.

"Hurry Amy, hurry," Parker urged.

Ty was already a quarter-way across the lake before Amy got underway.

When Amy and Parker reached the quarter-way mark, Ty didn't seem that much farther ahead.

26

In fact, he appeared to be slowing down. Amy and Parker were rapidly gaining on him.

"Uh oh. What's wrong now?" Ty said to himself. His skidoo's engine kept cutting out.

"What's wrong?" Amy asked as they came up beside Ty.

"The engine doesn't seem to be getting the gas; it keeps cutting out," he replied. "I think the gas line may be clogged."

"Maybe you're out of gas?" Parker queried.

"I can't be. We were full when we left the mine, and I haven't used that much," Ty replied.

"Amy, can you give me a hand?" he asked. "I'm going to clean the gas line."

"Sure," replied Amy as she dismounted from her skidoo.

"No sense all of us working on your skidoo. I'll just take this one for a little spin while you guys fix that one," Parker advised his siblings as he started the skidoo and took off.

Right from the start, he gunned the engine, and as before the track slipped on the ice. Try as he might, he just couldn't get the same traction that Ty got from his skidoo. It took him a while to pick up any speed. The track slipping on the ice frustrated Parker. He wanted to experience the same instant speed that Ty got from his skidoo. Looking towards

27

the shore, he realized the snow was deeper on the ground than it was on the ice. This would afford him better traction and better acceleration.

Soon he was tearing around on the shore, speeding up and slowing down, but he couldn't spin on the snow that was on the ground, unlike the wild, out-of-control spins the ice had to offer. While he enjoyed the exhilaration of quick starts, all thoughts of looking for the animal he had seen on the hill was forgotten. Instead, he focused his full attention on the skidoo he now had control of.

Ty got some tools out from under the skidoo seat, and lifting the engine cowling, started to work on the gas line.

"Boy, it's a good thing we had the safety course and Mr. Manik showed us how to fix these machines," Amy said.

"You're right. I wouldn't be able to do this if we hadn't had the maintenance course," Ty replied.

While Amy watched Ty work, her mind started to wander. She began to think of all that had happened since they'd arrived at the mine, and in her mind's eye she again could see exactly what had occurred.

chapter iii

WE'RE READY - let's go

At supper, Mr. Munro announced that he had set up the mine safety course for the next morning.

The kids couldn't believe their good fortune. They thought the course would be weeks or even a month or two away. But no, the day finally arrived just as Mr. Munro, the mine superintendent, had promised. They were going to take the safety course that would allow them to ride the mine's quads and skidoos by themselves. The kids could think and talk about nothing else.

*   *   *

Amy, Ty, and Parker were up early. No one wanted to miss the chance to qualify at the mine's safety course. The mobility course would offer the chance to explore the area they now found themselves in. It was something they could not afford to pass up.

Mr. Munro told them the mine safety officer was extremely busy and no one knew when the next course would be held. They would have to give the course their undivided attention because the opportunity to participate again would be a long time coming. The day held a lot of promise, and they couldn't wait to get started.

"Look! Look outside!" cried Amy. "It snowed last night."

"Good!" shouted Ty as he ran to the window. "The skidoos will work much better with more snow."

"The extra snow won't bother the quads, will it?" asked Parker.

"No, it won't bother them; it doesn't look like it snowed very much anyway," Ty remarked to Parker as he peered at the new snow on the ground.

"Hurry up, Mom and Dad," Amy called to her parents as she and the boys left their house for the kitchen.

The Trapps were to meet Mr. Munro and Bill Duncan, Max's assistant, in the kitchen. Then they would travel to the garage in Mr. Munro's company van.

"We're coming; right behind you," Max replied as the door closed behind Amy.

"Boy, they're really excited; usually they wait for us," Nadine, their mother, commented.

"Yes, they are. I can't remember when anything has had them as worked up as this safety course," their father replied.

"Well, you know what it is, don't you? If they pass the course, they think they'll be able to have the skidoos and quads to run all over the country. Other than getting the ice in the hockey rink, that's all Ty has been talking about," Nadine said knowingly as she smiled at her husband.

"Yes, I suppose you're right. Being at the dig all day, I miss a lot of their ramblings. It will be good for them to have the mobility the quads and skidoos will offer them. We'd better hurry; we don't want to be the ones who make the safety instructor wait," Max said with a laugh as he opened the door.

The rest of the group was in the kitchen when Max and Nadine arrived.

"I see we're all anxious to get started this morning," Mr. Munro remarked as he smiled and tilted his head towards the kids, busy devouring their breakfasts.

"As you can see, they even beat us out of the house," Max observed as he and Nadine took their places at the table.

"Come on!" Amy said to her brothers as she dashed to the kitchen door with Ty and Parker in close pursuit. They were in the van before the adults had left the table.

"We'd better get going or they'll leave without us," Mr. Munro chuckled as he rose from the table.

"Yep, they're pretty excited about the course," Max replied.

CHAPTER IV

ARE WE THERE YET?

"At last we're going to see the mine buildings and the pit," Amy said as she bubbled with excitement.

"I don't see what you're all hyped up about seeing the mine for. It's the skidoos and the quads I want to see!" Ty shouted.

"Well, we've only seen the mine buildings and the pit from a distance. We've never actually seen them up close," retorted Amy.

"What do you want to see, Parker? The mine and pit or the quads and skidoos?" Ty looked at Parker with a smirk on his face, like he knew what the answer would be.

"I'm looking forward to seeing everything.

The mine and the pit are going to give us something to look at, but the quads and skidoos are going to give us the freedom to explore. If Dad will let us, we'll be able to travel anywhere we want, once we've had the course," Parker observed.

"Yes, leave it to you to put everything into perspective. The mine and the pit are going to give us knowledge, and the quads and skidoos are going to give us freedom!" Amy smiled at her little brother.

Mr. Munro pulled away from the kitchen and the van started its one-kilometre journey down the bumpy gravel road. The kids' excitement was contagious and an air of anticipation filled the van as the journey continued. As the van crested the small hill between the kitchen and mine site, the huge garage, mill, and supporting buildings for the mines operation came into view.

"Is that the garage, the one the tent replaced?" Amy asked.

"That's it. Without this building we wouldn't have been able to put the tent over your dig site," replied Mr. Munro.

Whew, I thought the tent was big, but it's nothing compared to this," Amy exclaimed.

"Look at the size of the doors!" Parker shouted.

"Well, they have to be big to get our equipment in and out. The haul trucks alone are nearly three stories tall," Mr. Munro advised the group.

The kids stared in wonder at the huge structure before them.

"Are any of the big trucks in the garage?" Ty wanted to know.

"No, they're all in the pit. None are in for maintenance today," Mr. Munro answered.

"Are we going to go in through the big doors, Mr. Munro?" Parker inquired.

"No, there's a small garage door over on the side that I use; we'll go in that door," Mr. Munro replied.

"Oh," uttered Parker, sounding rather disappointed.

As the door opened and the van entered, Amy looked around in wide-eyed wonderment. "I thought the tent was big inside, but it's nothing compared to this. This is colossal!"

With none of the big equipment inside the garage, it looked even larger than it was. The little van that seemed to take up no room inside the huge garage made the group feel small and insignificant. 35

chapter v

safety first

Mr. Munro introduced the group to their instructor, the mine's chief safety officer, Johnny Manik. He had operated the skidoos and quads since the mine's inception and knew them inside out.

After the introductions, Mr. Manik presented each of the kids with a hard hat and a certificate certifying them as junior miners. The ceremony impressed the kids and they were made to feel like they really were a part of the mining crew. Mr. Manik advised them of the importance of having their hard hats on at all times to protect their heads. They wore their hard hats with pride and assured him they would wear them whenever they visited the mine buildings or the pit area.

With the introductions and ceremony at an end, the group moved further into the garage where Mr. Manik had two skidoos waiting for the students.

"When are we going to ride the skidoos, Mr. Manik?" Ty wanted to know.

"Have you ever ridden a skidoo before?" he asked Ty.

"Well no, I haven't, but it can't be that hard," Ty replied with a lot of confidence in his voice.

"Well, I want to show you some of the parts of the skidoo and what minor maintenance you should be able to do if you encounter any difficulties on the trail. Our safety course stresses that everyone who operates our equipment should be able to complete minor repairs," Mr. Manik informed Ty.

"What do you mean? What minor repairs will we have to do?" Amy asked.

"Come over to the skidoos and I'll show you," Mr. Manik replied as he walked towards the skidoos sitting in the garage. "Just form a semicircle around this skidoo and I'll explain what you are expected to know. We keep the skidoos in top working order. Some of the miners like to race them during their down time."

The kids formed part of the semicircle with their parents and Bill Duncan and gave Mr. Manik their undivided attention. Ty paid particular attention; he hadn't missed the part about racing the skidoos. He pictured himself racing against the miners and was sure he could beat anyone who dared to challenge him.

"I'll point out some of the parts of the skidoo so that you will be familiar with them," Mr. Manik advised the group. "These front runners are called skis. They are controlled by the handlebars and are used to control the direction the skidoo is going to travel. Above the skis is the engine cowling. It's on hinges and can be opened by unhooking these fasteners to expose the engine compartment. The body of the skidoo consists of the seat, which rests on the frame and is suspended above the track. The track is what the frame rides on and it in turn provides the traction that propels the skidoo forward. The seat is also on hinges and can be opened to reveal a small compartment where spare parts such as spark plugs and tools may be stored."

The kids were all eyes and stared intently at the skidoo as Mr. Manik explained the different parts of it.

"Do you have any questions?" Mr. Manik finally asked, looking from one to the other.

"Is this all we have to do with it? Just know the parts?" Ty asked.

"There's more we have to know, isn't there, Mr. Manik?" Parker queried.

"Yes, Parker, there is. You are expected to know how to clean and replace a fouled sparkplug and this is how you do it," Mr. Manik advised as he opened the engine cowling, revealing the engine, and then lifted the seat, exposing the compartment below. "This is a socket set. I'll need this to remove the sparkplug from the engine. If the sparkplug is fouled, I'll use this wire brush to dislodge any carbon or debris that is fouling it."

All eyes were on Mr. Manik as he removed the sparkplug, cleaned it with the wire brush, and then replaced it.

"Are there any questions?" asked Mr. Manik.

Everyone shook their heads in a negative manner.

"Good. Then there shouldn't be any trouble doing what I just showed you. Let's start with you, Amy. Everybody will have a turn doing what I just did." Mr. Manik stepped back to let

Amy at the skidoo for her first stab at maintenance.

Everyone took their turns removing the sparkplug, cleaning it, and then returning it to the motor.

"Boy, I'll bet that's the cleanest sparkplug in the world," remarked Parker as the last of the group completed their turn.

"Good work, everyone," said Mr. Manik. "Now let's move on to a plugged gas line and see if we can't unplug it."

Mr. Manik showed them how to disconnect the gas line from the carburetor and the gas tank. After showing them how to remove any blockages, he replaced the line and then had each of the group repeat the exercise. He also showed them how to repair and replace a track.

The difference between the quad and the skidoo for propulsion is that the quad has a gearbox and therefore you must change gears to make your quad go faster or slower. The skidoo, on the other hand, has a centrifuge clutch and to go faster or slower you must increase or decrease the throttle. Mr. Manik demonstrated how to start the skidoo and how it moves. He then started a quad and showed the group how to change the gears by working the gear shift with his left foot.

"These quads they're new, aren't they?" Max inquired.

"Yes, they are. They just came out last year. They replaced the ATV trike. The trike was very unstable and easily upset. They were going to stop producing them because of all the accidents they had. The manufacturers realized they had a good market for these small ATVs when they found out they were being used on farms and construction sites as well as for recreational purposes. The quads are much more stable. We wouldn't let the kids operate the trikes if we still had them. They were just too dangerous," Mr. Manik informed Max.

"I'm looking forward to riding one of the quads. I rode a trike before and as you say, they were very unstable. I'm not sorry to hear they discontinued making them," Max told Mr. Manik.

"I'm sure you will enjoy the experience, and I'm doubly sure the kids will enjoy them. Just from the expressions on their faces, you'd think they were already living the experience of riding one," Mr. Manik remarked.

The minor maintenance of the quad was basically the same as the skidoo, that being cleaning the sparkplug and clearing a plugged gas line. Everyone in the group took turns completing their assigned tasks.

Mr. Manik was satisfied that everyone who took the course was capable of operating and performing the minor maintenance as necessary. The time had come to take the units out for a test drive to show the instructor that they possessed the ability to handle the equipment safely and properly.

CHAPTER VI

WE'RE READY;
LET'S RIDE

The quads would be driven first, and Ty couldn't wait to showcase his abilities. He insisted that he go first. In his mind, there was nothing to this, and he would show the world that his driving abilities were second to none. Although he had never driven before, he was confident that he was probably an expert quad driver.

'Was that a look of pride or arrogance that flashed across Ty's face?' Amy wondered as Ty stepped on the footrest and swung his leg high over the seat while mounting the quad. No, she decided. It was just the excitement of the moment.

After starting his quad, Ty sat on it and revved the engine. Nothing happened, so he revved it some more. Thinking he wasn't giving it enough gas, he cranked the throttle wide open and the engine just screamed.

Amy and Parker were standing off to one side and watching the proceedings with interest. They couldn't see why Ty wasn't racing across the Tundra, the way his engine was running wide open, but he wasn't moving. He just sat there!

"What's wrong with this stupid thing? It won't go! Is it broken?" Ty asked Mr. Manik

"No, it's not broken. You don't have it in gear," replied Mr. Manik.

"Oh yeah, that's right. I forgot," Ty said as his cheeks turned red with embarrassment.

Ty was mumbling to himself as he put the quad in gear. In his embarrassment, he wasn't paying attention like he should have been. With the quad in gear, he revved the engine and popped the clutch. The quad leaped forward. The unexpected acceleration startled him and he almost lost control.

"Whoa!" Ty yelled, releasing the throttle, and the quad jerked to a stop.

This startled him more and he cranked open the throttle and shot forward again. He

46

repeated this bucking motion with the quad. He bounced across the tundra in front of the garage until he stalled it. To Ty, it felt like he had been on the quad for an eternity, but he had only travelled about twelve metres.

Amy and Parker were watching Ty's antics, and they couldn't contain themselves. They were both practically rolling on the ground with laughter.

"I'll bet you couldn't do that again if you tried," laughed Amy, tears rolling down her cheeks, while Parker nodded in agreement, unable to speak.

Mr. Manik could see that Ty was shaken up. He tried to make light of what had just happened so as not to embarrass him further. He assured him that this very thing happened to most people on their first ride.

Ty felt weak in the knees when he got off the quad. He was sure everyone at the mine was watching him, and his face was burning.

With a little further instruction, they were all riding with confidence and no further problems were encountered.

When it came time to ride the skidoos, Ty wasn't as forthcoming as he had been with the quads. He took a low profile and didn't insist on being first. He had learned that sometimes it is best to watch and listen.

Amy watched Ty closely and noticed that he wasn't as eager and confident as he mounted the skidoo as he had been with the quad.

Amy enjoyed riding the quads, but if she'd had her preference, she would have been doing something else like helping her dad at the dig. When it came time for her turn with the skidoo, her mind was someplace else. She wasn't paying attention when Mr. Manik told her about the power and the fast acceleration of the skidoos. She wasn't concerned because she knew the skidoos had a centrifugal clutch and therefore she didn't have to shift gears.

Starting the skidoo was easy. Absentmindedly, she twisted the throttle and the skidoo sprang to life. She wasn't expecting the next course of action. The handlebars she had been lightly grasping were ripped from her hands as the skidoo shot forward. She realized her mistake when her feet were going past her ears and she did a somersault off the back as the skidoo tore from under her.

She hit the ground with a thump on her rump. She was startled, and it took her a few seconds to realize what had happened. Everyone was staring at her with their mouths hanging open. They couldn't believe what they had just witnessed.

"Are you all right?" Nadine asked as she ran over to Amy.

"I – I'm fine, Mom," Amy said rather sheepishly as she looked around. "Don't you laugh," she scolded Ty and Parker, who were having a hard time containing themselves.

After Mr. Manik got them all going, he decided to take them on a little run to the lake ten kilometres west of the mine, where the miners fished during their down time.

All was going fine and it was a beautiful day for a ride. As they followed the leader heading towards the lake, Parker was congratulating himself on not pulling any of the boners that Amy and Ty had. He enjoyed a chuckle while recalling the antics that had been played out before him. He told himself he would have to remind the two just how funny they were. With his mind elsewhere, he didn't realize the lead skidoos had disappeared over the crest of the hill in front of him. He was soon to find out that the hill quickly dropped away down to the lake.

THE MINE

As he flew over the crest of the hill, his skidoo disappeared beneath him. He frantically tried to regain his senses but he seemed to be suspended in space. Jiminy-Willie-Peppers, what's happening? He wanted to scream. Before anything could come out, he was on his backside sliding down the hill behind his skidoo, which came to a stop when it reached the edge of the lake. He forgot all about reminding Amy and Ty of their funny predicaments as he regained his composure and sheepishly tried to laugh it off. Their situations didn't seem quite so funny now that he was in the same boat.

The kids had each experienced something they had not expected this afternoon, but they were not yet finished with new experiences.

"Did you learn from your mistakes?" inquired the voice through their Inuas.

"Kadluk, is that you?" the kids cried in unison.

"Yes, it is I," Kadluk's familiar voice responded.

"I think we all learned a lesson today," Amy remarked.

"It is good to learn. Remember, you are the shaman! When you are asked for help you must take

control of any situation. You must be the leaders," Kadluk reminded the kids.

"Kadluk, were you watching us today?"

There was no reply, only silence.

"Are you still here, Kadluk?" Amy inquired.

"He's gone again; he never stays long," Parker answered into the void.

The group returned to the mine site just in time to meet Mr. Munro and have the picnic lunch the kitchen staff had made for them.

chapter vii

the mine

"I'll give you a little history of the mine while we're enjoying our picnic," Mr. Munro informed the Trapps. "A number of years ago, an enterprising fellow discovered what he thought were Kimberlite Pipes in this area. These pipes are believed to be ancient volcanoes and were first discovered near Kimberly, South Africa. That's how they got their name. Diamonds are formed under great pressure and temperature deep in the interior of the earth. They are brought to the earth's surface through Kimberlite and Lamproite Pipes. Three pipes were discovered under a shallow lake where we presently have our mine. Three years ago, we brought in equipment and drained the lake."

"You drained the whole lake?" uttered an astonished Parker.

"That's right, and since then we have been building our mine. We have about two years to go before we'll be at full production. Right now we're at about sixty percent capacity. We're still building up our site and it takes a while as everything comes in prefab on the resupply ships in the summer. It takes time to prepare all the sites we need for our buildings.

"I don't know if you noticed," Mr. Munro continued, "but all our buildings are raised approximately four feet off the ground and all are on gravel pads called berms. It's necessary to do this because we're on permafrost. If we put a building directly on the ground, the permafrost would melt and the buildings would sink."

"What is permafrost?" asked Amy.

"It's ground that is permanently frozen. Most of the tundra is made up of permafrost. It is a vast treeless Arctic region. If you were to draw a line from Inuvik, Northwest Territories, to Churchill, Manitoba, just about everything east of this line would be the Tundra or the Barrens, as it is commonly called. West of that line would be the tree line," replied Mr. Munro as he continued with his talk.

"What are those wooden boxes that connect the buildings?" Ty inquired.

"Those are called utilidors. It's a Canadian invention. When you're on permafrost, you can't bury your water pipes, sewer pipes, etc. These utilidors are heated and insulated wooden casings. They are approximately two feet square and run to all the buildings and they carry all the pipes above ground so that they don't freeze," Mr. Munro answered.

"That's kind of neat," Parker remarked.

"How many miners work here?" Amy asked.

"Right now we have about 250 employees. In two years, when we're at full capacity, we'll have about 325. The miners work twelve-hour shifts, twenty-four hours a day, seven days a week. They work two weeks on with one off. We never shut down except for maintenance or weather," Mr. Munro replied.

"I never realized your staff was that large. You're going to have a little town yourselves when you're fully operational," Max remarked.

"Yes, it takes a lot of work to build and run a mine this size," Mr. Munro informed the group.

"What are we going to do next, Mr. Munro?" Amy asked.

54

"Don't you think you've done enough for today, my dear?" Nadine interjected.

"Oh, no, Mom. We want to see the mill and the pit. Don't we, boys?" Amy excitedly cried, looking at her brothers.

"Yeah, there's lots we haven't seen. We haven't even seen one of the haul trucks yet!" shouted Parker.

"When we've finished our picnic, we'll take a tour of the pit and the mill," Mr. Munro informed the smiling kids.

chapter viii

the pit

It was a short one-kilometre drive from the garage to the pit. As they went over the lip of the rim and started the descent into the pit, Amy said, "Look how big the pit is. I never realized that it would be this big...This is huge!"

"It's not very big yet, little lady," replied Mr. Munro. "We're just getting started. In a couple of years this pit will be five times the size it is now, with twice as much equipment working. As you can see, the floor of the pit is relatively flat. We've only got two levels going right now, but we'll have three eventually. We start in the middle and just keep expanding the hole until we've reached the outer walls of the Kimberlite Pipe. As the top level is exhausted, we'll start another hole in the centre and create another level. Each level is about fifteen metres deeper. We don't like to get much more difference in height than that as the haul trucks can easily handle a load up that type of grade. There's no reason to put extra strain on the equipment, especially in these harsh conditions, when we don't have to."

"This is awesome," Ty said as he viewed the huge haul trucks that dwarfed the van they were riding in.

Mr. Munro pulled up beside the haul truck that was waiting its turn to be loaded. He had called the haul truck driver on his CB and he was waiting for them.

"Anybody want to take a look inside the cab of the haul truck?" Mr. Munro asked the group.

"I do! I do!" shouted Ty.

"Me too!" cried Parker and Amy.

The kids were out of the van before it came to a complete stop.

"I don't even come up to the hubs of these wheels!" Ty exclaimed as he looked up, viewing the massive tires that supported the truck.

"How tall are the tires, Mr. Munro?" Parker asked.

"They're twelve feet high. Pretty big, aren't they?" Mr. Munro replied.

"They sure are!" exclaimed Amy.

"Come around to the front and we'll take the stairs to the cab," Mr. Munro said to the group.

As the group walked up the stairs to the cab, Ty remarked to Parker, "Wouldn't it be fun to drive one of these babies on the road?"

"I don't know," said Parker. "I don't think they go very fast and they're so big they'd take up the whole road."

"Yeah, I guess you're right, but I still think it would be fun," Ty muttered rather dejectedly.

Each of the kids took turns sitting in the driver's seat and pretended to be driving as they turned the big steering wheel from side to side.

"Look!" cried Amy. "The van we were in is so small I can't even see it from here! I can just see the flag on the top of its mast."

"Yeah, you're right! So that's what the flag on the mast is for," Ty responded as he tried to see the van from the cab of the haul truck.

"That's right," Mr. Munro responded. "Without that flag, the haul truck drivers wouldn't know there was a vehicle below them."

"This is something the kids won't forget for a long time," Max advised Mr. Munro as they descended the truck's stairs.

"Anything that will bring them enjoyment and give them an experience they won't forget is reward enough. It's tough being stuck in a lonely place like this with very little to do for youngsters their age. I just hope they have enough to do and don't get bored while they're here," Mr. Munro remarked.

"From what I can see, they seem to be adjusting very well to the place and are enjoying everything so far," Max replied.

"Good. Anything we can do to keep them busy and happy will be done," Mr. Munro informed Max.

"Oh, I think you're doing more than enough, and I thank you," Max replied.

From a safe distance, they watched as the giant walking dragline dug the diamond ore from the ground and piled it where the loaders could load it into the haul trucks. In addition to the haul trucks and dragline, the kids were amazed by the other equipment in the pit. There were blasthole drills, bulldozers, loaders, and hydraulic backhoes with an assortment of other support equipment.

"I've never seen trucks as big as that before," Parker muttered to no one in particular, staring in wonder at their size.

"Yes, that dragline and the loaders can keep all the trucks hopping when they're running at full speed. Just a word of caution: never come into the pit unless you're with one of the miners or myself. These trucks could run over you and never even know it," Mr. Munro said as he started up the ramp to leave the pit.

*   *   *

"Bang!"

Amy jumped a foot in the air.

"What's that?" she yelled as Ty slammed the engine cowling back into place.

"What's the matter? Did I scare you?" Ty asked. He laughed at the startled look on Amy's face.

'How do I totally recall the incidents that have taken place?' Amy wondered to herself. It was the same as the experience she'd had when they were having their lunch. She knew it had something to do with her Inua, but what it was she didn't know. Her Inua was allowing her to recall experiences exactly as they had already occurred.

chapter ix

my head hurts

Ty mounted the skidoo. "Just let me get this baby started and then we can head home," he said to Amy.

Parker, meanwhile, was still tearing around on the shore. He didn't see the rock that was higher than the rest of the terrain. The rock was snow-covered and even if Parker had been paying better attention to what he was doing, it would have been hard to detect. He never saw it coming. The right ski hit that rock with a bang and stopped dead in its tracks, torn from its housing.

"What was that?" Ty and Amy said in unison, turning towards the shore, just in time to see Parker's skidoo do a crazy spin.

"Whoa!" screamed Parker as he sailed through the air, doing cartwheels, having been ejected from the skidoo.

Then the sickening screech of metal on rock could be heard. Ty likened it to someone scraping their fingernails down a blackboard. He winced and a chill ran down his spine as the heavy skidoo's rear end rose in the air and swung around. As though in slow motion, he and Amy watched it slowly turn over and come crashing to earth upside down. "Whomp," they heard as it hit the ground and skidded backwards on the shore.

When the skidoo's right ski hit the rock and the skidoo spun around, Parker was thrown from the skidoo and soared high into the air before being flung to the ground.

"Oof," was all Ty and Amy heard as the air was forced from his lungs when he landed and lay still.

Ty was running as hard as he could towards his little brother. "Parker! Parker! Are you all right?" he yelled.

Amy knew Ty was fast, but she'd never realized how fast he really was. He was at Parker's side before she had covered half the distance, and they had started at the same time.

"Is he okay?" Amy yelled to Ty.

Parker lay motionless, and Ty checked his pulse.

"I think he's just knocked out," Ty replied, "but I don't like the way his right leg is bent." Parker's leg was underneath him; he'd landed on it when he hit the ground.

"I don't like the looks of it, either," Amy stated, kneeling at his side. "Do you think it's broken?" she asked as she looked at her little brother.

"We won't know until he wakes up, but we don't dare move him," Ty replied.

"What should we do now? It's going to be dark soon. You're going to have to go for help. We can't possibly all ride on the one skidoo in the condition Parker is in," Amy said.

"You're right, but we'll have to get him off the snow. I can take the track off the broken skidoo and we can use it as a mattress for him, just to get him off the ground," Ty answered.

"I'll stay with Parker; you get the track," Amy replied.

Ty was gone in a flash while Amy worried about her little brother.

"Oh, my head hurts," Parker moaned after several long moments.

"Parker…Parker, can you hear me?" shouted Amy.

"Of course I can hear you. Quit shouting; my head hurts," Parker moaned.

"Can you move, Parker?" Amy shouted again.

"What happened?" He moaned again.

"You had an accident with the skidoo. You hit a rock," Amy advised him.

"Oh, my head hurts. We should have brought the amulet, Amy," Parker cried out.

"Yes, we should have. It's my fault. This wouldn't have happened if we'd had the amulet with us," Amy stated.

"It's not your fault; we all forgot to bring it," Parker weakly replied.

"Lie still. Ty went to get the skidoo track for you to rest on. He's going to go for help. We all can't ride on the one skidoo," Amy told Parker.

Ty soon returned with the skidoo track and they moved Parker on to it.

"How's your leg?" Ty asked.

"It's sore, but I can move it. I don't think any bones are broken."

"I'm going now; I'll be back as soon as I can," Ty said as he turned toward his skidoo.

"Hurry Ty, but be careful. We'll be waiting for you," Amy advised her brother.

Ty and his skidoo were soon speeding across the lake and disappearing from sight, heading for home and help.

*   *   *

The daylight was more than half gone when Kadluk finished with his furs. This trip had been successful and he was happy with his bounty. It was time to check on the weather and see if he could find out anything further on the blizzard Sila had eluded to earlier.

When he went outside, he found the wind gently blowing and everything quiet and calm. Although the weather was serene, he felt there was now a crisper, colder feel to it. He had to know if the storm was coming.

On the light post next to Kadluk's residence perched a large raven. He was staring at Kadluk intently as if wanting Kadluk to ask him something.

To Kadluk, the raven is the creator and he often lets Kadluk use his eyes to see that which he cannot see himself. As long as Kadluk can see the

67

raven, he can use the raven's eyes to see things many miles away that he cannot see from where he's standing.

"*Can I use your eyes?*" Kadluk asked the raven through his Inua.

"*Yes, you can. What do you wish to see?*" the raven replied.

"*I heard Sila talk of a blizzard. I want to know if it's coming this way,*" Kadluk told the raven.

With a quick hop off the post, the huge shiny black raven rose in the air. Its beautiful black wings lifted it higher and higher. Up, up went the raven, but still Kadluk could see nothing out of the ordinary. All was as it should be.

"*Perhaps the blizzard is occurring elsewhere,*" Kadluk said to the raven's Inua.

"*I will go a little higher,*" said the raven, and up he went.

"*What's that over those far-off hills to the north?*" Kadluk asked, but he didn't need an answer. He could see the blizzard coming like a steam-rolling snowball that stretched from horizon to horizon, as far as the eye could see. The monster was consuming everything in its path. The howling winds that were pushing this beast would have it here within the hour.

Kadluk said to the raven, *"You'll have to find shelter. This looks like a bad storm. I'm lucky I came home last night and can enjoy the comfort of my house until it blows over.*

"Are you finished looking through my eyes?" asked the raven.

"Yes, thank you. Wait a minute…What's that over west, on the lake?" Kadluk asked. He had just caught a glint of sunlight reflecting off shiny metal.

"It appears to be a skidoo on the lake," remarked the raven.

"Yes, that's what it is, but there's another skidoo upside down on the shore of the lake. I see three people, and one is lying down and appears hurt."

Kadluk had a sickening feeling in his stomach. He recognized his young friends immediately. He knew instantly they didn't have the little amulet with them and were therefore not protected. Otherwise, Parker would not be lying on the ground hurt. Sitting out the storm in the comfort of his house was now a thing of the past; he must act quickly if he were to save his young friends.

"I can't get to them before the blizzard strikes. See the herd of caribou bedded down on the other side of the hill from them? Can you ask the caribou to bed down

around the Kabloonas to protect them until I get there?" Kadluk asked the raven.

"Of course I can," replied the raven, and he took off flying northwest towards the herd.

Kadluk knew Ty would be going for help and that he would be travelling southeast until he hit the Meliadine River, then following the river east until he hit the winter road that joins the mine to Rankin Inlet. He would then follow the road to the mine. He would have to act quickly if he were to catch Ty before he got to the winter road. He might never find it in the blizzard that was fast approaching.

Kadluk knew that Ty's chance of survival was slim or none at all if he didn't find him before the blizzard engulfed him with all its fury. Kadluk could find someone who was stationary, but finding someone moving around in a blizzard was something else, and he shuddered to think of his young friend in this situation. Although this trio of young people possessed the abilities of a shaman, they still had lots to learn.

Kadluk quickly packed his komatik. The fastest dog team in the land had been resting since last night and was ready to go. One crack of the whip and the slack leads went taut. The komatik was flying over the frozen tundra, on its mission of mercy.

*   *   *

The raven approached the caribou herd and landed on the back of a small caribou. *"Who speaks for this herd?"* he asked.

"I speak for this herd," replied a large caribou.

"Can you bed down on the other side of this hill to the east?" asked the raven.

"We could. It matters not where we bed down. Why do you ask?" queried the caribou.

"It matters not to me, but there are some young Kabloonas on the other side of the hill near the lake who need protection from the coming storm," the raven told the caribou.

"Why do you concern yourself with protecting the young Kabloonas?" the caribou wanted to know.

"I am not concerned, but THE OLD ONE asked me if I would ask you to protect the young Kabloonas from the coming storm. He's on his way but can't get here before the storm hits," the raven advised the caribou.

"THE OLD ONE has always shown the proper respect to all living things, and we will do as he requests," the caribou stated.

71

*   *   *

Although the caribou had never seen THE OLD ONE, they knew it was an honour to even be asked to help. They had heard the Tungat, the deities who control the number of animals in the Inuit world, sing his praises. No living being shows more respect for everything in his world than THE OLD ONE.

The herd had been listening to the Creator and the lead caribou converse. They rose as one and headed east over the low-lying hill.

"Oh, my head hurts," wailed Parker again.

Amy was concerned about her little brother. Nothing she did seemed to comfort him. She was going to have to think of something to get his mind off his suffering. She wished Ty were still here, but she knew he was rushing to seek help.

Crunch-crunch-crunch, came the unexpected sound.

"What's that, Parker? Can you hear it?" cried Amy.

"I don't know what it is," replied Parker.

Just then the herd of caribou crested the hill and moved towards them. The whole side of the hill seemed to be moving as the large herd approached.

"We're going to be trampled!" cried Amy.

"No, they're not stampeding. They're just walking," Parker advised his sister. "Talk to their Inua, Amy. Make sure they know we're here."

"Why are you coming here?" Amy asked the caribou through her Inua.

"We are coming to protect you," replied the lead caribou.

"Protect us from what? We don't need protection," Amy scoffed.

"Amy, look!" Parker cried as he pointed north.

As Amy looked, the giant wall of snow came swirling towards them, driven by the howling wind.

"Oh no, look at that!" Amy cried.

The caribou surrounded Amy and Parker to shelter them from the howling wind and the blanket of snow that engulfed all in its path. The larger caribou stood next to Amy and Parker, then the smaller ones, with the last ones lying beside them. This created a snug den between the caribou that sheltered the kids from the blizzard.

"Who would have thought the caribou would do something like this? This is just like being in a cave and covered with a big hairy blanket," Parker marvelled.

"Yeah, and it's warm too. It beats being exposed to what's raging around us," Amy replied.

In spite of their protection, Parker began to feel tired and scared.

Amy noticed that Parker was starting to weaken. She didn't want him to fall asleep. "Parker, remember the first time we visited the mill?" she queried.

"Kind of," Parker replied.

"I remember it well," Amy informed Parker, "I'm going to remind you of what happened."

Chapter X

A Race Against Time

Ty had just reached the Meliadine River when he noticed the wind was up and a few snowflakes were falling. He turned east when he arrived at the river. This turn caused him to look over his left shoulder, and he got the first glimpse of the monster that was pursuing him. It stretched from horizon to horizon and was hungrily devouring everything in its path as it continued its relentless march southward.

His hopes sank. He had a long way to go before he would reach the mine road. He thought to himself, 'I've got to keep ahead of this. I'll never find my way if it catches up to me.' The sight of the monster caused him to accelerate in his desperate effort to stay ahead of being consumed by the boiling snow. Fear was now driving him in his mad dash for safety. His thoughts went immediately to Amy and Parker. How could they survive this storm, alone, without shelter on the barren lakeshore?

He hadn't traveled a mile down the river when he observed the dog team heading towards him. Who would be crazy enough to be out with this storm blowing? Surely the musher could see the storm brewing. He should be camped waiting out the storm. What was he thinking?

Nonetheless, the sight of another human gave him immediate comfort. A closer look at the fast-approaching musher told him he was coming face to face with Kadluk. The relief he felt when he realized it was THE OLD ONE was immeasurable, and he talked to Kadluk through his Inua.

"What are you doing out here?" Ty asked.

"I've come to help you. Quick, get off the skidoo and get on the komatik. We have no time to lose," Kadluk replied.

One doesn't argue with Kadluk. Ty did as he was told and they were soon flying over the tundra to rescue Amy and Parker.

Only Kadluk could take on a storm of this size with confidence. The storm was of no consequence now, and Ty felt safe and secure as Kadluk drove his dog team headfirst into the raging storm.

*   *   *

Amy and Parker were enjoying the comfort the caribou shield offered.

Amy's mind recalled everything that had occurred during their first trip to the mill. Using her Inua, Amy related the following to Parker.

Round

Oval

 *Heart*

Pear

Emerald

Marquise

chapter xi

the mill

A short drive brought them to the mill, just west of the huge garage. On the north side of the building, they could see where the haul trucks dumped the concentrate.

"Why are the trucks dumping the ore there?" asked Amy

"It has to be crushed before being taken inside the mill on the conveyor belt so that it can be fed into the cyclones," Mr. Munro advised his young friend.

The children were familiar with cyclones from the times they'd spent in the tropics. They had no problem recalling the screaming winds accompanied by the torrential rains brought on by cyclones. Visions of vicious storms, with giant trees being torn out by their roots and flung vast distances, raced through the minds of the kids, as did houses being torn apart by gale force winds and the countryside awash with the floods that followed. Cyclones were something they knew all about and wanted no part of.

"Wow! Jiminy-Willie-Peppers, I don't want anything to do with cyclones!" exclaimed Parker.

"Remember that one we were in in New Guinea? Remember how hard it rained and how the wind just screamed?" Amy recalled.

Mr. Munro could see the kids were uncomfortable at the mention of cyclones. "It's not what you're thinking," he told them. "Come; I'll show you," he said as they entered the mill.

The kids conversed through their Inuas.

"Do you think Mr. Munro could understand what we were talking about?" Amy queried Ty and Parker.

"No, he couldn't have! Kadluk said he doesn't have the traits of a shaman," Parker answered.

"Well, it was just the way he looked at us…Like he was reading our minds or listening to us," Amy said.

"Don't forget, he's mined all over the world and has probably been in a number of tropical storms,

including cyclones," Parker reminded his two siblings.

"Yes, I should have known you would remember that point. You're probably right as usual, Parker. He just guessed what we were saying because of his many travels around the world," Amy offered.

"Look over there," Mr. Munro said, pointing to his right. "That's where the diamond-bearing concentrate is fed into the cyclones after it has been crushed. We use the cyclones to extract the diamonds by mixing diamond-bearing concentrate with a fluid near the density of diamond. Separation occurs in cyclones by swirling the mixture at high velocities. Fast rotation of the suspension drives heavy minerals to the conical wall. There, they sink to the bottom and are extracted, while float waste minerals are sucked from the center of the vortex. Cyclones are about 99.999% efficient at extracting diamonds and similarly dense minerals from the original ore. That's pretty well it in a nutshell; it's really quite a simple procedure."

"When you explain it like that, it's a lot less complicated than it looks," replied Max.

"What happens to the diamonds after you get them out of the cyclone?" asked Amy.

"After the extraction, they're sorted into three groups. 'Sizes' are more than one carat, 'smalls' are between one carat and one-tenth of a carat, and 'sand' is less than one-tenth of a carat. A carat is a unit of weight of precious stones," Mr. Munro explained. He continued, "Diamonds are weighed in carats and points. One carat equals 200 milligrams and one point equals 0.01 carat. The ultimate purpose of sorting is to estimate an asking price for the rough diamonds. Diamonds larger than fifteen carats are handled individually. There are five shape groups and they are comprised of stones, shapes, cleavages, macles, and flats," he finished.

"Are they used for anything besides jewelry?" asked Ty.

"They certainly are. A diamond is the hardest substance known to man. In 1812, the German mineralogist Frederich Mohs devised a scale of mineral hardness. Using different minerals, he determined which was harder by the minerals being able to scratch or mark each other. If one mineral wasn't able to scratch another mineral, it was determined to be softer on the scale.

"On the Mohs scale for hardness," Mr. Munro continued, "a diamond is 10. The next hardest substance known to man is corundum and it is 9 on the scale. A diamond is 4+ times harder than corundum on the Mohs scale. It has the highest refractive index of any natural mineral. It is the best conductor of heat and has the highest melting point of any substance. Its melting point is 4090° C. Furthermore, no substance affects diamonds. It is the most inert and durable of any material. Diamonds are very rare, and due to their brilliance and hardness, they are the most famous of all gems. Only about twenty percent of diamonds found are of gem quality. The other eighty percent are used as abrasives, as thermal insulators, in optics, in electronics, etc.," Mr. Munro advised his listeners.

"How do you know if your diamonds are of gem quality?" asked Amy.

"All rough diamonds are classified by weight, shape, clarity, and color," he answered. "In the final analysis, diamonds can be sorted into more than 14,000 categories. The colors of diamonds are graded on a color scale established by the Gemological Institute of America. The scale ranges from D, which is colorless, to Z, which has a brownish hue. Other diamonds with hues of pink, blue, green, yellow, and very rarely red are referred to as fancy diamonds. Fancy diamonds are considered extremely rare," Mr. Munro finished.

"*Did you hear that?*" Amy asked Ty and Parker through her Inua. "*Mr. Munro said a red diamond is the rarest diamond of all!*"

"*So what?*" Ty replied.

"*Don't you remember? Kadluk said his grandfather had a red diamond,*" Amy responded.

"*That's right, and he said he'd show us where his grandfather found it. Didn't he, Amy?*" Parker asked.

"*He didn't say he would; he said he might someday,*" Ty clarified.

"*We'll have to tell Kadluk the red diamond is the rarest of diamonds,*" Parker quickly added.

"*I doubt it will matter to him, but we can tell him,*" Amy remarked. "*Now pay attention to what Mr. Munro is telling us,*" she told her brothers.

"*Okay, Amy,*" Parker replied.

"Why do they say, 'Diamonds are a girl's best friend'?" Amy queried Mr. Munro.

"I really don't know the correct answer to that question, but it could be for a number of reasons. It could be because diamonds seem to last forever. They were formed up to three billion years ago deep in the earth and brought to the surface some seventy million years ago by volcanic eruption. It could also be because they were first found in India about four thousand years ago and because of their luster and hardness were thought to possess magical powers. Leaders and religious persons kept them as sacred objects or important treasures. Some, who thought they would lose their power if they were altered in any way, used them as talismans. A talisman is a good luck charm and it is believed by the wearer to ward off evil spirits. Sometime during the eleventh century, they started to be worn as jewelry. During the thirteenth century, people discovered they could enhance the beauty of diamonds by grinding and polishing them. Later, diamonds became the symbol to sanctify and solidify the union of marriage. They represent eternity, fidelity, and love. It is believed that the first engagement ring was given to Mary of Burgundy by Austria's Archduke Maximilian in 1477," replied Mr. Munro.

"With all the categories that you mentioned, if you were going to buy a diamond, how would you pick out the one you wanted?" asked Amy.

"That's very simple, my dear. I would follow the guide of the 4Cs and that means cut, color, carat, and clarity. This guide is used throughout the world to classify the rarity of diamonds. Therefore, the diamonds with the highest 4C rating are rarer and more expensive," Mr. Munro informed the group.

"Are diamonds all cut the same?" inquired Parker.

"No. Generally speaking, there are seven principal diamond shapes for jewelry, as well as some side stone options. The main forms are round, marquise, emerald, princess, pear, oval, and heart.

The round is the most popular; three out of four stones will have this shape," replied Mr. Munro.

"How many diamond mines are there in Canada?" asked Amy.

"This is the first of what I'm sure will be many to come in the years ahead. Testing so far has yielded evidence of a wide area of Canada that should contain Kimberlite Pipes. We are on the threshold of Canada becoming a major supplier of the world's diamonds. Our mine so far has shown that we will produce superior gem quality diamonds," answered Mr. Munro.

"Well, you've certainly given us a lot to think about, Mr. Munro," Amy told him as the group left the mine.

CHAPTER XII

YOU FOUND US

Amy finished relating the story as it had unfolded.

"How did you do that, Amy? How did you recall everything like that?" Parker wanted to know.

"I don't know. It's something to do with my Inua, I think, but I really don't know. It seems if I start thinking about something, my Inua can replay it for me."

"What's that?" asked Parker suddenly.

"What's what?" queried Amy.

"I thought I heard dogs barking," Parker replied.

"I don't hear anything. If there were dogs, the caribou would be running," Amy observed.

"No, I think I heard something," Parker again stated.

"How could you hear anything above the roar of the storm?" Amy wanted to know.

"Ask the caribou if they heard anything," Parker insisted.

Using her Inua, Amy talked to the caribou.

"*Mr. Caribou, can you hear anything? My brother thinks he can hear dogs barking.*"

"*Your brother is right. I can also hear the dogs,*" the caribou stated.

Why aren't you running away from the dogs?" Amy asked.

"*Because we were asked by THE OLD ONE to protect you until he arrives and that is what we are going to do,*" replied the caribou.

"*Is it Kadluk? Has he come to save us?*" shouted Parker.

"*Yes, it is THE OLD ONE. You will now go with him,*" the caribou informed the kids. Upon saying that, the caribou herd parted and let Kadluk and his dog team reach Amy and Parker.

"*Boy, am I glad to see you,*" Parker said to Kadluk and Ty as they loaded him onto the komatik.

"*Quick, everyone on the komatik. We have no time to lose!*" Kadluk commanded.

"*How are you feeling, Parker?*" Ty queried.

"*I'm okay, but my head hurts,*" Parker replied.

"Kadluk, how did you know we were in trouble?" Amy wanted to know.

"It matters not; you are safe now," Kadluk remarked.

Knowing Kadluk, Amy knew that would be the only answer she would receive. Kadluk was not one to elaborate on anything. He did what had to be done without any fanfare. If anything further had to be told, it would be told at a feast where Kadluk would be in his element as he regaled his audience with a live performance of any event worth relating.

The blizzard raged on, but the kids were now snuggled in the furs on the komatik and Kadluk was mushing his dog team towards the shelter and safety of the mine. Once again, all was well.

*   *   the end   *   *

GLOSSARY

Inua – (inh' oo ah) n, the spiritual occupants, or spirit helpers, that reside in all living or inanimate things

Inuktitut – language of the Inuit

Kabloona - white man

Komatik - (koh-ma-tik) n, sled with wooden runners and crossbars bound with animal hides

Shaman - (sham-man) n, 1 a priest of shamanism. 2 a medicine man or witch doctor of a similar religion. (They have special abilities in relating to the supernatural powers)

Sila - an all pervasive spirit that resides in the air

Tungat - (plural of tungak) the spirits who control the supply of game animals

ACKNOWLEDGMENTS

My son was the driving force behind this endeavour and still keeps me on track as the works progress. If any credit is given it must go to him as this project would never have been undertaken without him. His illustrations capture the essence of the stories.

My brother is living proof that a brother can be your best friend. His encouragement and timely advice has helped me avoid many pitfalls in the self-publishing industry.

A special thanks to Dianne Hawkins and to Maureen Pedersen who have helped me improve my grammar in some of the books.

I must thank my family for allowing me the huge amount of time it takes to complete a task of this undertaking. Without their help and encouragement none of this would see the light of day.

The Author

Lawrence was born and raised in Alberta. 37 years of his adult life was spent serving in the Canadian Armed Forces and the Royal Canadian Mounted Police. The author draws on 10 years of living in the Yukon and the Northwest Territories for the inspiration for his stories. Retirement finds him again in Alberta where he presently lives with his wife Judith. They have 2 children and 6 grandchildren.

The Illustrator

Rob Adams, son of Lawrence Adams; when he is not working on his fathers illustrations, can be found working on game designs. Trained in Visual Communication, Rob currently works in the field of video games, juggling roles of a producer and game designer. Rob has had first hand experience of living and visiting many of the places described in the Trapps Family Adventure books.

Other books by Lawrence E.R. Adams.

the old one
the amulet
the stolen soul
the creator
the amulet

Watch for future books by Lawrence Adams as the
Trapps Family Adventures continue to explore the
mysteries of the north.

who walks on my land
who swims in my waters
who flies in my skies
the spirit of marble island
the search for the red diamond
the little people
the rescue

Join Amy, Ty and Parker as they continue to seek
answers to life's adventures on the frozen tundra.

GIVE A "**LAWRENCE E.R. ADAMS**" BOOK TO A FRIEND

Trapps Publishing
P.O. Box 212
Irricana, AB T0M 1B0
www.trappspublishing.com
Send to:

Name:_____

Street:_____

City:_____

Province/   Postal/

State:_____Zip Code_____

Please Send:

"THE OLD ONE"	____	X @ $9.95 =_____
"THE AMULET"	____	X @ $9.95 =_____
"THE STOLEN SOUL"	____	X @ $9.95 =_____
"THE CREATOR "	____	X @ $9.95 =_____
"THE FAMINE"	____	X @ $9.95 =_____
"THE MINE"	____	X @ $9.95=_____

Shipping and handling for first book @ $4.00
plus $1.00 each additional Book (Shipping and
handling free in Canada and Continental USA)   =_____

5% GST =_____

Total amount enclosed: _____

Make cheque or money order payable to:
TRAPPS PUBLISHING
Price subject to change without prior notice.
ORDERS OUTSIDE OF CANADA must be paid in U.S. funds
by cheque or money order drawn on U.S. or Canadian Bank.
Sorry no C.O.D.'s.